A Funny Sort
of Minister

A Funny Sort
of Minister

Dominique Demers

Translated by Sander Berg

Illustrations by Tony Ross

ALMA JUNIOR

ALMA BOOKS LTD
3 Castle Yard
Richmond
Surrey TW10 6TF
United Kingdom
www.almajunior.com

A *Funny Sort of Minister* first published in French as *Une drôle de ministre*
by Éditions Québec Amérique in 2001
This translation first published by Alma Books Ltd in 2019
© Dominique Demers, 2001

Translation © Sander Berg, 2019

Inside and cover illustrations by Tony Ross. Illustrations first published
in France by Éditions Gallimard Jeunesse
© Éditions Gallimard Jeunesse, 2006

Printed in Great Britain by CPI Group (UK) Ltd, Croydon CR0 4YY

ISBN: 978-1-84688-456-6

Contents

Prologue

Miss Charlotte is an old lady who doesn't do anything like other people. In *The New Teacher* she gets her pupils to use spaghetti as a ruler, in *The Mysterious Librarian* she arranges books by colour, and in *The New Football Coach* she teaches young footballers how to lose.

There are many people who think that Miss Charlotte must be totally bonkers because she talks aloud to Gertrude, her rock. But children in loads of schools, towns and countries who have got to know Miss Charlotte now chat to their toothbrushes or tell their secrets to a pebble.

A Funny Sort
of Minister

Chapter 1

Time to Be Reunited with Gertrude

With a pounding heart, Miss Charlotte studied the train timetable in the central station. "In two hours and fifty-four minutes. At last!" she sighed, putting down her elephant-skin travel bag.

In two hours and fifty-four minutes she would be boarding a train that would take her to Saint-Anatole. And in Saint-Anatole she would be reunited with Leo, Marie... and Gertrude! Miss Charlotte knew that Leo and Marie were taking good care of her precious Gertrude, but, after giving it a lot of thought, she had come to the decision it was time for her to be reunited with her great friend.

With a spring in her step, the old lady walked towards the ticket window, leaving behind her travel bag. Right in the middle of the busy train station! Miss Charlotte could be a bit of a scatterbrain sometimes...

That very moment, a few streets away, a loud noise made a number of passers-by jump into the air. A car tyre had burst. And not just any old car tyre! It was the rear tyre of the limousine belonging to the Prime Minister, Roger Rarejoy.

The Prime Minister's driver immediately got out to check the damage. His aide got on his mobile to order a new limo, while his body-guard stepped out to make sure no one would bother the Honourable Roger Rarejoy.

The Prime Minister had been in the middle of going over a speech he was going to give to the APWTTAVVI (Association of People Who Think They Are Very, Very Important) at the Coliseum later that day. It was a unique occasion, a historic moment. Before an audience of a thousand people, and with nine television cameras and sixteen radio microphones pointing at him, he was going to reveal the key policy of his election manifesto: a new educational programme for children.

Roger Rarejoy had got to the second paragraph of the third page, a key passage that would turn the lives of all the children in the country upside down. It said that breaks would be abolished, that children would even have to go to school on Saturdays and that the summer holiday would be reduced to two weeks per year. Instead of playing football in the park, camping, cycling or swimming in swimming pools and lakes, the children would spend nearly the entire summer in the classroom.

Before he had finished reading this paragraph, his aide Simon Surenough informed him that all the roads were blocked because of a massive strike by truck drivers. If the Prime Minister wanted to get to Saint-Mealymouth by ten past ten for the opening of a new biological onion farm, his only option was to take the train. And quickly!

Ten minutes later the Prime Minister, with his aide and bodyguard, arrived at the station, all out of breath. While Simon Surenough ran off to get the tickets, a lady asked the Prime Minister for his autograph. Roger Rarejoy put down his old elephant-skin travel bag in which he kept all his important documents. It had been a gift from his favourite Auntie Josephine, and he never left home without it.

While Roger Rarejoy was speaking to his admirer, other people recognized him too, and in the blink of an eye a big crowd had formed around him. At that moment Miss Charlotte saw the Prime Minister's bag and picked it up, thinking it was hers. She hugged it and said, gently stroking the elephant skin:

"My poor little baby! I thought I had lost you."

To celebrate being reunited with her bag, Miss Charlotte decided to treat herself to a big bowl of noodle soup at the station restaurant. She was already on her way when Roger Rarejoy discovered that... his bag had

moved. It was no longer at his feet but right in the middle of the hall!

The Prime Minister ran over to pick it up. Without losing a second, he opened it and let out a cry of horror.

Miss Charlotte was about to sit down at her table when she realized something was not right: her bag was too heavy. So she opened it to check.

"Great grasshoppers' bottoms! This bag is full of stuff!" Miss Charlotte cried out.

That was indeed remarkable and highly unusual, seeing as Miss Charlotte was in the habit of stuffing her travel bag with... nothing at all! That is how it seemed, at least. But on her travels Miss Charlotte had collected lots of memories that were extremely precious to her, invisible though they were.

Miss Charlotte rummaged around in the bag until she came across a leather-bound diary carrying the initials: P.M.

P.M.? Miss Charlotte wondered who this unknown individual whose bag she had inadvertently picked up might be. Could he be called Paul Michaud? Pamphilius Mirabilius? Philip Macadamia? She opened the agenda and discovered the address of this mysterious P.M. It was 8 Deluxe Street.

How convenient! Miss Charlotte had crossed that street on her way to the station. With a bit of luck she could return the bag to

P.M., get her own back and still make her train. She would have to skip her noodle soup, though.

"Poor little pumpkin! We'll have to make it up to you later," she said, patting her tummy, which was so hungry it was making loud engine noises.

Chapter 2

Gustave-Aurèle Brillantine-Rarejoy

On 8 Deluxe Street there stood an imposing mansion surrounded by a tall iron fence with spikes on top. Miss Charlotte did not allow herself to be intimidated. She walked straight to the entrance and gave the bell three long rings.

Gerald Gardiner, the butler, opened the door and frowned when he saw this strange, very tall and very skinny old lady wearing a bizarre kind of hat.

"Who can I say is there?" he asked in a stuck-up voice.

Émeline Brillantine, the Prime Minister's wife, had told him that she was expecting a new tutor to teach her son Gustave-Aurèle. She must have made a mistake, because this was clearly a tutoress or, erm... tutrix. And really looking rather... Well, you know...

"Is this where Paul Michaud lives?" Miss Charlotte asked.

She struggled to contain her giggles, because Gerald Gardiner sported a huge moustache which reminded her of a bushy skunk's tail.

"Or maybe Pamphilius Mirabilius?" Miss Charlotte continued.

The butler's moustache trembled as if it were alive. Miss Charlotte felt like laughing out loud.

"Paulette Marabout? Petronilla Marcilla? Penelope Macadamia?" she went on.

The butler wrinkled his nose in disdain, which made his moustache jump up and down. Miss Charlotte burst out in giggles.

Gerald Gardiner immediately decided that this strange kind of madwoman could not possibly be a tutor, and without further ado he shut the door in her face!

"Phew! My tutor has not arrived yet," Gustave-Aurèle Brillantine-Rarejoy said, delighted, having watched the whole scene from his window on the third floor.

A nearly twelve Gustave-Aurèle had had an unbelievable number of tutors. Tall and skinny ones, short and fat ones, and even little skinny ones and tall fat ones. They all had their tics. The first was always chewing toothpicks, while the last would pick his nose behind an exercise book. In the eyes of Gustave-Aurèle's parents, none of them were good enough. Roger and Émeline wanted nothing but the best for their son. They were keen for Gustave-Aurèle to excel in music and physics, as well as languages and maths.

Gustave-Aurèle was jealous of the other children. They played football in the street, ate chips with gherkins and watched horror films on the telly. Meanwhile, *he* spent his

days swotting up on his school subjects, having music lessons, learning about IT and perfecting his chess moves. The worst of it was that even though he worked his socks off, he always had the impression it wasn't good enough.

Gustave-Aurèle was about to leave his observation post by the window to get back to his geometry when Miss Charlotte began to sing at the top of her voice and horrendously out of tune. It was her way of dealing with frustration. Then she did some dance steps in the middle of the road, followed by a pirouette. To finish it off, she roared like a gorilla with a tremendous toothache.

"That did the trick!" she said, happy to have regained her good mood.

That's when Gustave-Aurèle noticed that the strange visitor was leaving with his father's travel bag, a very rare piece that had been given to him by his dear Auntie Josephine, who had disappeared during an expedition to Mount Python.

The Prime Minister's son was well behaved and orderly, and not at all prone to impulsive actions. But when he saw his father's priceless travel bag being carried off like that, he decided to act. And on the double!

"It's ten past nine… The butler will be in the entrance hall, the chambermaid outside the dining room and the other maid at the bottom of the stairs," Gustave-Aurèle thought to himself. So he rushed to a room at the back of the house, opened a window, climbed down the fire escape ladder and ran after Miss Charlotte as fast as his legs could carry him.

Chapter 3

Long Live Saint-Citron!

Miss Charlotte slurped down her third bowl of noodle soup while Gustave-Aurèle – for the first time in his life! – tucked into a huge slice of pepperoni pizza.

They had returned to the station in the hope of finding Roger Rarejoy still there, but the Prime Minister had already left. Miss Charlotte then invited Gustave-Aurèle to accompany her to the station restaurant.

"Are you sure your father is the Prime Minister?" asked Miss Charlotte when she had finally eaten her fill.

CHAPTER 3

Gustave-Aurèle swore he was telling the truth. Miss Charlotte really surprised him. She had never heard of the Prime Minister or his political party. She travelled with an empty bag and talked out loud to objects. She had also had plenty of adventures. Everything she said, did and thought fascinated the Prime Minister's son.

Gustave-Aurèle realized that Miss Charlotte was not a thief. She had simply picked up an elephant-skin travel bag that was identical to hers. How Roger Rarejoy must have panicked when he discovered that instead of containing all his important documents his bag contained nothing but air!

"Look!" said Gustave-Aurèle, opening Roger Rarejoy's agenda on 8th May. "My dad had something on in Saint-Mealymouth this morning. Now he is on his way to a car factory in Saint-Citron. And then, this afternoon, he is meeting some fishermen in Port-Folio, and this evening... Oh no! This evening my dad is due to present his new policy on children's education. There will be loads of people, and he will need his papers.

"Really? And what is this new policy?" Miss Charlotte asked.

"I have no idea," Gustave-Aurèle admitted.

"Are you telling me that your father did not ask your advice?" Miss Charlotte said, sounding surprised.

"Of course he didn't. I'm a child!"

"Exactly! Did you not say that this new policy was about the education of *children*?"

Gustave-Aurèle thought Miss Charlotte had a point. He would have been delighted to give his opinion.

"What if we looked in the bag... The policy document is probably in there somewhere," Miss Charlotte suggested, dying of curiosity.

"No! We don't have the right to do that," Gustave-Aurèle cried out, horrified. "We need to get on the first train to Saint-Citron. That way we'll be able to return all the papers to my dad. For once he will be proud of me. He may even offer you a post in his Cabinet."

Little did Gustave-Aurèle know that things would turn out rather differently. As for Miss Charlotte, she realized she had a new mission. Gustave-Aurèle needed her. And besides, if there was a chance the Prime Minister might offer her a job...

Miss Charlotte began to daydream about the positions she would like to occupy. She did not have the foggiest about how to govern, but she knew she would be the

happiest woman alive if the Prime Minister
asked her to cultivate woodlice or spiders,
or to invent a new type of noodle, or design
humongous sand castles...

Chapter 4

The National Guide to Healthy Eating

"What!? You're *lost*!?" the Prime Minister's aide hollered into his mobile.

He could not stop shouting at the driver of the car sent by the national security forces to pick up the Prime Minister from the train station at Saint-Citron. That banana-brain had lost his way and crossed the wrong bridge.

Roger Rarejoy was not too bothered by the setback. He had had enough of presentations and exhibitions, of official openings and declarations. His precious bag was full of documents that were really very urgent. And yet his advisers were always getting him to take part in a whole range of activities just to get his photo in the papers.

The Prime Minister gently stroked the empty elephant-skin bag, thinking about his Auntie Josephine. She was the only one who would listen to him. The only one, too, who ever spoilt him. Roger Rarejoy sighed when he thought of the treasures she had given him in secret. Little bags filled with things his parents would not let him have: liquorice, fudge, jelly beans and, above all, sweet bombs that burst in your mouth and turned into fireworks.

Roger Rarejoy blushed deeply. Thinking about those sweets had made him very hungry. He would have given his gold watch for a handful of sweet bombs. But he knew that as a result of a new policy on child welfare, put together at the request of a pressure group, sweets had recently been banned.

Chapter 5

The Prime Minister Is Useless!

"We're there!" Miss Charlotte shouted with joy while crossing the street energetically.

Gustave-Aurèle was amazed. That asparagus of a woman was incredibly fit. He himself was out of breath after running from the station to the factory, hoping to get there on time.

About a hundred people were gathered in a hall of the ZWZ factory at Saint-Citron. They were waiting for the Prime Minister to finally show up to unveil a new type of car that was standing there, covered by a large canvas.

"My dad is late. I hope nothing has happened to him," Gustave-Aurèle whispered to Miss Charlotte.

At that moment, the director of the ZWZ factory, a little bald man who was sweating profusely, walked up to the microphone, followed by his director of communications, a woman in heels that were so tall it looked like she was walking on stilts.

"I regret to inform you that the Prime Minister has been held up," the little bald man began.

A howl of protest arose from the crowd. Everyone was very disappointed.

"Aw shucks! And I was so looking forward to seeing him in person," a pretty lady told her friend.

"That goes to show that the Prime Minister is rubbish!" an old man shouted. "A good thing I didn't vote for him."

"Well, he certainly isn't very reliable," someone else added.

Gustave-Aurèle had steam coming out of his ears. He wanted to tell everyone that they were wrong to criticize his dad. The Prime Minister surely had an excellent reason why he could not be there. Roger Rarejoy worked hard. Very hard! So hard, in fact, that he suffered from high blood pressure, indigestion, palpitations, infections and other ailments.

Suddenly a murmur spread through the crowd. Gustave-Aurèle turned to Miss Charlotte... only to discover she was gone!

Chapter 6

The 24–RP3

"We have just been told that the Prime Minister has sent us a representative," the director of communications in her high heels said into the microphone. "It will be Miss… erm… Charlotte?!… who will do the official unveiling."

"Oh no! God help us!" Gustave-Aurèle muttered to himself.

Miss Charlotte walked up to the microphone with a beaming smile and greeting the crowd as if she were a film star.

"Hello everyone! Welcome! Bienvenue! Hola! Aloha!" she said cheerfully.

The director of communications in her high heels scanned the crowd with a worried look. She reckoned the Prime Minister could have found someone a bit less... or a bit more... Anyway... But to her great relief the people seemed to find her amusing. Miss Charlotte's good humour was contagious.

CHAPTER 6

Miss Charlotte had never been to an unveiling. She had no idea about what she was *supposed* to do. But she knew what she *felt* like doing.

Miss Charlotte had always dreamt of being a singer. Unfortunately for her, she sang out of tune and sounded like a croaking toad.

"I'd like to start off with a song," she improvised.

"Oh no! Will someone please help us?" Gustave-Aurèle thought to himself.

Seeing the look of panic on the face of the director of communications, Miss Charlotte realized that one is not supposed to start an unveiling ceremony with a song.

"I was only kidding," she said, in an attempt to recover.

At that moment, Miss Charlotte noticed that the little bald man, whose head was covered in big beads of sweat, was pointing at a cord. She pulled it. Immediately cries of "Oh!" and "Ah!" came from the crowd as the cover came off, unveiling the new model car from the ZWZ factory: the 24–RP3.

It was a tiny purple car that looked kind of cute. The director explained that the car ran on water, which made it the most economical and least polluting car on the market.

"I now hand over to the most distinguished representative of our esteemed Prime Minister," he said before stepping aside.

"Oh no! Help! Please? Anyone?" Gustave-Aurèle repeated to himself.

Miss Charlotte walked up to the microphone.

"If the 24–RP3 runs that well on water, imagine how it will run on lemonade or Ribena," she said with the most serious face in the world.

The guests laughed heartily, without Miss Charlotte really understanding why. She did not know what else to say, apart from the fact that she thought that for such a pretty little car the 24–RP3 had a pretty awful name.

What would be a better name, Miss Charlotte wondered calmly, while the eyes of the whole crowd were fixed on her. Then she spotted Gustave-Aurèle among the guests. Gustave-Aurèle...

Miss Charlotte suddenly had an idea. Gustave-Aurèle... G-A... GA... GA... Without giving it any further thought, she announced:

"In honour of the son of our Prime Minister, Gustave-Aurèle, who is here with us this morning, I have the tremendous honour of renaming this lovely little thing 'GAGA!'"

The hall remained silent. No one knew what to make of this announcement.

"Just looking at it makes you go completely gaga," the fake representative of the Prime Minister said, before letting out a bellowing laugh.

Miss Charlotte's sense of humour was a bit... peculiar. Plus, she laughed like a sea lion. But she laughed with so much gusto that her joy was infectious. Little by little, the people in the crowd joined in, and soon the whole hall was roaring with laughter. In the end Miss Charlotte received a thunderous applause.

"I'd vote for her!" one of the people next to Gustave-Aurèle said.

"Me too!" added his friend. "She's a lot less boring."

Chapter 7

No Way We'll Pay a Ransom!

"It's terrible! Horrendous! Absolutely disastrous!" Simon Surenough cried out.

Roger Rarejoy was even more shaken. Having missed the previous two engagements, they were now on their way to Port-Folio in the new limo when they heard the devastating news on the radio.

On the news at noon the newsreader mentioned that a certain Miss Charlotte had stood in for the Prime Minister at the ZWZ car factory. To start with, the PM did not have a representative to stand in for him. To make things worse, the newsreader said that, given the huge popularity of this mysterious old lady, people were speculating whether she might soon become a minister or an MP.

Roger Rarejoy's aide nearly choked on his tie when he heard these words. Could Miss Charlotte be in cahoots with Victor Vigour, the opposition leader?

The Prime Minister was worried for a different reason. He had been given quite a shock when he heard that Gustave-Aurèle had been present at the Saint-Citron factory.

Roger Rarejoy immediately phoned 8 Deluxe Street, where Gerald Gardiner, the butler, had discovered Gustave-Aurèle was no longer in his room. He also mentioned the visit of a strange old lady earlier that morning. Twelve minutes later the secret service confirmed that the description of this curious visitor matched that of the fake representative.

"She has kidnapped the Prime Minister's son! That loathsome creature will be demanding a ransom," Simon Surenough said. "We need to find her! Our Government will not give in to blackmail."

Roger Rarejoy did not usually stand up to his top advisers, but this time he could not stop himself.

"I want my son back! Even if it costs us millions. Gustave-Aurèle is my son!"

The shock had made Roger Rarejoy realize that his son was a billion times more precious to him than his elephant-skin travel bag and all the important documents in it.

Chapter 8

Her Majesty's Tea

"You really shouldn't have... You did not have the right..." Gustave-Aurèle kept telling Miss Charlotte.

They had stopped in a park and were sitting next to a pond. Gustave-Aurèle was sitting on the grass and took great care not to get his trousers dirty.

Miss Charlotte looked at him calmly. She did not give a hoot whether he was the son of the Prime Minister or of a window cleaner. What bothered her was that Gustave-Aurèle did not look happy.

"OK, sure!" Miss Charlotte admitted. "I should not have walked up to the microphone, and I have no right to go around renaming cars. But I cannot say I am sorry I did it – I would happily do it again."

Her grey-blue eyes looked straight into Gustave-Aurèle's.

"Are you always this well behaved and perfect?" she asked him gently.

"Me? Erm… Well, yes… Of course…" Gustave-Aurèle stammered.

A mysterious smile spread across Miss Charlotte's lips. Gustave-Aurèle had the impression that she looked straight through him – that she knew his innermost secrets and could read his deepest thoughts.

"Just tell me…" Miss Charlotte said, trying to encourage him.

Gustave-Aurèle lowered his eyes. He was not sure what was happening to him. He suddenly felt like sharing everything with this strange old lady whom he barely knew. He had the feeling he could tell her anything, and that his secrets would be safe with her.

For about an hour Gustave-Aurèle poured his heart out to Miss Charlotte. He told her that he was often bored, that he felt ever so lonely and found it very difficult to live up to his parents' expectations. He wished they would pay a bit more attention to how he felt, to his dreams and fears, rather than his tutor's latest report.

As he was talking, Gustave-Aurèle felt as if a great burden had been lifted off his chest. In the end he confessed to his elderly friend that he was not always as perfect as he appeared to be. He had even played some... naughty pranks. In secret, of course.

"Because I'd had enough," he admitted.

The first time was after he had been forced to eat snails with mushrooms and mustard at an official dinner at Buckingham Palace. Gustave-Aurèle had courageously swallowed these horrid rubbery grey things. But he had taken his revenge.

He waited for the perfect moment when everyone was talking about politics and money, and then he poured vinegar into the Queen's tea! Oh, the memory of it! Gustave-Aurèle squirmed with pleasure as he watched the Queen take a sip. At first she grimaced, but then she smiled and… drank it all!

After that, he had fun sprinkling sugar on the President of the United States' ravioli and daubing toothpaste all over the King of the Can-Can

Islands' seat. Once he also flung dog poo into the next-door garden so that the butler would step into it. One day he even slipped three spiders' legs into the corned-beef sandwich of his most detested tutor.

Miss Charlotte had to bite her tongue at that last confession, because she adored spiders.

"I've done worse," she said, without even blushing.

Gustave-Aurèle watched his new friend closely. He felt she was speaking the truth. All of a sudden he decided to tell her about his worst exploit.

"One day I stuck my dad's toothbrush in the toilet bowl!"

Miss Charlotte did not seem impressed.

"I've done worse," she simply said.

"Tell me…" Gustave-Aurèle pleaded.

So, to please her young friend, Miss Charlotte told him about the worst trick she had ever played. She had written a false weather forecast announcing forty centimetres of snow. Not a single snowflake fell, but three thousand three hundred and thirty-three pupils enjoyed a whole day off school.

Gustave-Aurèle was flabbergasted. Miss Charlotte really did have some cheek.

"I've done all sorts of silly things," Miss Charlotte admitted. "Sometimes I've gone too far, especially when I was angry. But I don't get angry any more, because I discovered a trick."

"What trick?" Gustave-Aurèle asked.

"I sing!" Miss Charlotte replied. "And it works! Within a few seconds, my anger is gone, and I am happy again. It does not matter what I sing or where I am, or how I sing or who is there... The sadder or angrier I am, the harder and louder I sing. And if things get really bad, I dance as well."

To convince her friend, Miss Charlotte began to sing at the top of her lungs, and horrendously out of tune, not giving a fig about the looks she got from passers-by.

"I believe you! I believe you!" Gustave-Aurèle assured her, to make her stop.

Unfortunately Miss Charlotte did not feel like stopping at all.

Chapter 9

The Children of Yakou Bourou

"It's a disaster!" Miss Charlotte concluded in horror.

To Gustave-Aurèle's huge despair, she had been rummaging in the Prime Minister's bag and had opened a document that said "ultra-secret" on it. It was, of course, the infamous new education policy.

Miss Charlotte had read it lying on her back in the grass next to the pond. Gustave-Aurèle had read it too.

The Prime Minister's son was disappointed. In front of a thousand people, nine television cameras and sixteen radio microphones, his dad was about to reveal a policy that would condemn all the children in the country to a life of boredom.

"We need to prevent that from happening!" Miss Charlotte said, with anger in her voice.

Gustave-Aurèle did not know what to think of all this. His dad was surrounded by top advisers who could hardly be wrong about these things. The new policy was the result of a trip the Minister for Education, John Genius, had made to Yakou Bourou, a little island in the Egyptian Sea. There he discovered that the children study ten hours out of twenty-four, six days out of seven and fifty-two weeks a year. They also only eat red meat, white fish and green vegetables. And they are top performers in all school subjects.

Gustave-Aurèle was still mulling this over.

"My dad knows what he is doing," he said. "The proof is that the children from Yakou Bourou do much better than we do."

"Maybe..." Miss Charlotte admitted. "But I am sure they are not as happy."

Gustave-Aurèle lowered his eyes.

"We absolutely have to rewrite the children's education policy," Miss Charlotte decided.

"Oh no! God help us!" Gustave-Aurèle thought to himself.

He was expecting Miss Charlotte to get to work immediately. Instead, she stretched herself out on the grass like a cat, breathing in the scent of lilacs.

"I shall first have a little break, followed by something to eat," Miss Charlotte announced. "After that I always work better."

Gustave-Aurèle studied his new-found friend. Sometimes he had the impression she was the most sensible grown-up he had ever met. At other times he was not so sure...

Chapter 10

I Want My Son Back!

Miss Charlotte and Gustave-Aurèle had been fooling around in the pond, splashing each other and throwing up roasted peanuts and catching them in their mouths. Lying on their backs now, Gustave-Aurèle was looking for animals in the clouds, while Miss Charlotte was dreaming up a recipe for noodles with crème fraîche and poppies.

Meanwhile, the secret service were looking everywhere for the mysterious fake replacement. An identikit photograph had been sent round to all police stations. Miss Charlotte was accused of impersonating someone else, stealing valuable documents and kidnapping a minor!

Sitting in a large upholstered armchair in his office, which was the size of a small ship, Roger Rarejoy was biting his thumbnails, a sure sign of how incredibly nervous he was. He had just told his wife about the disappearance of their son. Émeline Brillantine had immediately cancelled the talk she was meant to give to the AVVLW (Association of Very, Very Liberated Women).

"That criminal shall soon be arrested, handcuffed and put in prison," Simon Surenough promised the Prime Minister. "The important thing to do now is to get ready. In three hours and thirty-three minutes you need to give your speech. Don't forget to put on your blue tie – it's the one that looks best on you."

"I won't say a word in front of a microphone before I've got my son back," the Prime Minister said, offended.

Simon Surenough looked outraged, but for once Roger Rarejoy did not allow himself to be intimidated.

"Please leave my office," he ordered, "I have to think."

Alone at last, the Prime Minister thought about how fond he was of his son. In two days Gustave-Aurèle would turn twelve. Already! Roger Rarejoy remembered his own twelfth birthday. He had spent some magic moments with his dear Auntie Josephine!

They had spent the night dreaming up stuff, laughing and chatting. At sunrise they had treated themselves to spaghetti with honey and oranges. Afterwards they had slept in a tree hut they had built on the shore of Grasshopper Lake, until their tummies woke them up. Then Auntie Josephine had shown him how to build a proper fire with wood so they could grill sausages and roast marshmallows on sticks.

The Prime Minister let out a deep sigh. What he wouldn't give to relive that day! But it was impossible, of course, because he had become a reliable, respectable, reasonable and reserved man.

At least, that's what he thought...

Chapter 11

It's Raining Stars

"What do you think?" Miss Charlotte asked.

Gustave-Aurèle's mouth was wide open. He had just read the new policy his friend had written. It was totally outrageous, one hundred per cent unthinkable and... utterly wonderful!

Her policy stated that children must absolutely learn how to blow bubbles with their chewing gum before the end of Year 7. It was equally important to learn how to climb huge trees, to build your own kite, to lose yourself in funny or terrifying books, to raise exotic animals and to invent extravagant dishes...

Miss Charlotte also mentioned the need to do sums and write correctly, but she did not spend much time on that bit. "Happy children learn quicker and better," she simply wrote.

"I can't wait to present my ideas to the thousand delegates!" said Miss Charlotte, her eyes shining with delight.

Gustave-Aurèle felt he needed to prevent her from doing just that. At the same time, he did not really want his dad to give his

speech either. If only the event could be cancelled!

"If I could convince my dad I was in mortal danger," he thought, "he might cancel his speech."

The trouble was that he was not sure. What if his dad decided that his role as Prime Minister was more important than the well-being of his child?"

Suddenly Gustave-Aurèle had an idea. A truly daring plan.

"We have a little time left before the meeting. What would you like to do?" asked Miss Charlotte, putting her notes in order.

Gustave-Aurèle was so used to just studying and working that he did not really know what to suggest.

"How about telling each other stories?" Miss Charlotte proposed. "What's your favourite story?"

Gustave-Aurèle thought about it. He was torn between the life of Napoleon and the life of Caesar. The son of the Prime Minister only knew stories that had really happened.

"The Vikings!" he finally told her.

"Oh yes! Tell me..." Miss Charlotte urged him, her eyes wide with excitement.

Gustave-Aurèle described the cruel expeditions of the Vikings, those fearsome pirates who ploughed the waves with their dragon-headed ships.

"They were greedy and knew no mercy," he explained to his elderly friend, who was very impressed. Those sea bandits burned,

pillaged and killed, terrorizing people wher-
ever they went.

After a few minutes Gustave-Aurèle stopped.
He had told her as best he could all that he
knew about the subject.

"Continue," Miss Charlotte insisted. "It's
fascinating!"

"That's all they've taught me. I'm sorry…"
Gustave-Aurèle said apologetically.

"So? Make it up!" Miss Charlotte suggested,
as if that were the most obvious thing to do.

Gustave-Aurèle nearly choked.

"You can't just make it up. This is about what
really happened!"

"Oh, I see… Well, invent another story then,"
Miss Charlotte suggested.

Gustave-Aurèle felt as if she had asked him
to jump off a tall bridge.

He knew how to study, memorize, observe,
calculate, summarize… But to invent? Not a
chance.

"You're having me on," Miss Charlotte
protested. "That can't be right… Don't tell

me you've never invented a story just for yourself."

She could not believe it. She felt very sorry for the Prime Minister's son.

Miss Charlotte gave her young friend a long, piercing look.

"What would you like to be?" she asked him. "In which period would you like to have lived? Which galaxy would you like to explore?"

Gustave-Aurèle's eyes widened in amazement. Miss Charlotte continued: "Would you like to kill a dragon with a sword? To transform yourself into a leprechaun, a giant or a sorcerer? Would you like to swim with dolphins? Gobble up clouds? Fly on the back of a bird with wings as large as gliders?"

Gustave-Aurèle had gone pale with desire. He wanted to scream: "YES!!!"

"You can!" Miss Charlotte assured him. "All you need to do is use your imagination…"

The Prime Minister's son was dazed. It seemed too fabulous to be true.

CHAPTER 11

Miss Charlotte decided to help him.

"Close your eyes," she said. "Trust me."

Gustave-Aurèle closed his eyes, trembling a bit.

"Now listen," Miss Charlotte said very gently. "It's easy. You always begin with 'Once upon a time'. Here we go… Once upon a time… there was a boy called Gustave-Aurèle who was fed up of always being alone and sensible.

"One night, after an incredibly boring dinner party at the house of the Grand Poohbah of Yakou Bourou, Gustave-Aurèle was woken up by a terrible noise.

"The window of his room was wide open. The curtains were flapping wildly in the wind. The sky was purple, and it was raining stars.

"Gustave-Aurèle heard a deep, hollow voice.

"'I am right here,' the voice said.

"At that point Gustave-Aurèle saw a gigantic hand appear at the window. He

got closer and saw an extraordinary creature, the like of which he had never seen
before.

"Gustave-Aurèle climbed onto the window
ledge and, without hesitation, jumped into
the open hand…"

Chapter 12

Bossanova and Marimba

"I can see them now! They're in Bossanova Street, near Boyer. Request immediate back-up," police officer ZO-ZO whispered into a microphone in his watch as he climbed down a stepladder.

Gustave-Aurèle and Miss Charlotte were on their way to the Coliseum and had not spotted the police officer disguised as a window cleaner. His colleague, police officer NO-NO, who pretended to be a traffic warden, was supposed to intercept the Prime Minister's son and his kidnapper a bit further along, on the corner of Bossanova and Marimba Street.

Gustave-Aurèle walked briskly. In his head he kept going over his plan. He needed to be courageous and not lose his calm if he wanted to outsmart the security guards and set off the fire alarm. If he was successful, the Coliseum would be evacuated and the speech postponed to another day.

"In ten seconds," agent NO-NO whispered in his watch, just as Miss Charlotte and Gustave-Aurèle were walking straight towards him.

Suddenly Miss Charlotte stopped in her tracks. She had spotted a small fragment of a light-blue ribbon on the pavement. It was all dirty, grotty and frayed. And just when agent NO-NO wanted to grab her, she went over to one side, knocking over a few passers-by without meaning to, and delicately lifted up the string of ribbon.

"Poor darling! You're all used up! Don't worry... I'll take good care of you," she said with a sweet voice.

Gustave-Aurèle would have given anything for the earth to swallow him up there and then. The passers-by were laughing and pointed their fingers at that strange old lady who spoke aloud to a ribbon and stroked it as if it were alive. To make things worse, soon horns were beeping loudly because Miss Charlotte was blocking the road.

Then Gustave-Aurèle spotted the man standing behind Miss Charlotte. He was talking into his watch. Discretely. Ever so discretely.

In a flash Gustave-Aurèle understood the situation. It was a police officer. They were looking for Miss Charlotte! He should have thought of that.

"Help!" he cried in a panic.

Miss Charlotte turned to Gustave-Aurèle. Agent NO-NO did the same, as did all the passers-by.

Gustave-Aurèle had a brilliant idea.

"Help! That man is mad! He's after me!" he screamed, pointing at agent NO-NO.

He took Miss Charlotte by the arm and off they ran, as fast as their feet could carry them.

"What a monster! Attacking a child like that!" the outraged passers-by cried out as they closed in on agent NO-NO.

"Maximum alert! I think they're on their way to the Coliseum," agent NO-NO was nevertheless able to communicate via his watch to the head office of national security.

Chapter 13

Pizza and the Police

Miss Charlotte and Gustave-Aurèle were hiding underneath a stack of pizza boxes in the back of Antonio Tortello's van. The delivery man for Mamma Pizza had kindly offered to help them.

"Look out! Don't move!" Antonio warned them when a police officer signalled him to stop.

By order of the national security office, all vehicles on their way to the Coliseum had to be checked. The police officer opened the back of the van to have a look inside.

That's when Antonio noticed that Miss Charlotte's boots were sticking out from underneath the pizza boxes!

"You wanna slice offa da pizza?" he offered the police officer, opening a box wide and so hiding Miss Charlotte's boots.

Delighted, the police officer walked off with a slice of pepperoni pizza. A few minutes later Antonio let his passengers out at the entrance to the Coliseum.

Miss Charlotte and Gustave-Aurèle managed to slip into the building without being noticed, because Gustave-Aurèle had had the brilliant idea to borrow Antonio's peaked cap to disguise Miss Charlotte. With her own large hat, the old lady would have been arrested on the spot.

The Coliseum was chock-a-block. The Prime Minister was looking at the audience on one of the security monitors. He recognized Victor Vigour, the opposition party leader, Gilly Gender, a journalist with the CACO, Raymond Ragout, who wrote for the OGPT, and, all the way at the back in the corner... Gustave-Aurèle!

A huge smile spread across the Prime Minister's face. Not only was Gustave-Aurèle alive and well, but he was laughing his head off.

You should know that Miss Charlotte had just given him a riddle. What is yellow, red and white and goes up and down? When he heard the solution – a banana dressed up as Father Christmas in a lift! – Gustave-Aurèle thought it was such a stupid joke that he burst out laughing.

Roger Rarejoy had a close look at that oddball Gustave-Aurèle was having so much fun with. Her pizza-delivery cap, her dress and… her elephant-skin bag!

The kidnapper!

The Prime Minister felt as if he had been struck by lightning. Still, he really did not feel at all like alerting the security services.

"That woman does not look dangerous. She even reminds me of someone…" Roger Rarejoy thought.

Suddenly he cried out: "Auntie Josephine!"

His advisers quickly turned towards him. What on earth had got into the Prime Minister?

Roger Rarejoy was moved.

He knew his Auntie Josephine had dis-appeared trying to reach the summit of Mount Python. But this old lady looked so very much like her. So awfully much! So marvellously much!

Without warning his advisers, the Prime Minister walked out of the wings and onto the stage, towards the microphone. Not because he was about to give his speech, but because he felt he needed to have a closer look at the woman in whose company his son seemed so happy.

Gustave-Aurèle saw his dad move in their direction. At the same time, Miss Charlotte had started to walk towards the stage. She had made up her mind to present her own programme.

Gustave-Aurèle understood that this was the moment to set his plan in motion. He located the nearest fire alarm and dodged two security guys by zigzagging between the legs of delegates of the APWTTAVVI

(Association of People Who Think They Are Very, Very Important). Then he stood on the tip of his toes and put his hand on the fire-alarm button.

All of a sudden "Ohs" and "Ahs" started coming from the crowd. Gustave-Aurèle did not budge as he watched Miss Charlotte walk straight up to the Prime Minister.

"What's happening to me?" Gustave-
Aurèle wondered, with his hand still on
the button.

He felt unable to set off the alarm. And it
was not because he lacked courage. Gustave-
Aurèle Brillantine-Rarejoy had just realized
that he had changed in the course of that day.
So much so that he no longer felt like pre-
venting Miss Charlotte from giving her talk.

To his great distress, he saw four security guys close in quickly to intercept Miss
Charlotte as she was about to step up to the
stage. At that moment Roger Rarejoy's voice
rang out in the room.

"No! Stop! Let her talk!"

Chapter 14

Simply Happy

Miss Charlotte did not manage to convince the thousand members of the APWTTAVVI that it was absolutely essential that all children learnt how to blow bubbles with their chewing gum by the end of Year 7. But they listened attentively as she presented her policy on the education of children.

Once she had delivered her talk, Miss Charlotte told three awful jokes, and she could not help but finish it off with a little song. The delegates thought she was highly amusing. They were convinced Miss Charlotte sang like a croaking toad on purpose. Her good humour and sweet madness had rapidly won them over.

Deep down, without being aware of it, they were tired of being serious. All they really wanted to be was simply happy.

While Miss Charlotte was entertaining the crowd, Gustave-Aurèle and his dad had gone backstage, away from everyone else. Roger Rarejoy hugged his son for a long time. After that, Gustave-Aurèle told his dad everything he had learnt since Miss Charlotte had entered his life.

Father and son agreed that the educational policy for children would be rewritten to include not only time to work, listen and study, but also to build tree huts, invent stories and eat explosive sweets that turn into fireworks. Roger Rarejoy also promised Gustave-Aurèle to tell him about Auntie Josephine, his favourite aunt.

Gustave-Aurèle wanted to give the good news to Miss Charlotte. But when he came into the auditorium he discovered that... his elderly friend had disappeared!

A few minutes earlier, Miss Charlotte had waved goodbye to the audience as if she were a film star and had stepped off the stage. No one had seen her since.

Epilogue

Later that same day, Roger Rarejoy and Gustave-Aurèle found the infamous elephant-skin bag filled with important documents in the huge office of the Prime Minister. Miss Charlotte had added a letter.

Dear Mister Roger
Prime Minister,
I no longer want to be involved in politics, but I would like to make one small suggestion. I think the best place for you to think about your brand-new and ever so admirable educational policy for children would be a hut among the trees on the shore of the beautifully named Grasshopper Lake.

A thousand hugs to your son Gustave-Aurèle – who, in my opinion, would be a great help with the job.

Miss Charlotte

PS: *And lots of kisses to you too!*

THE END

"She's bonkers!"

Miss Charlotte, the new teacher, is not like the others: she wears a large hat and a crumpled dress that make her look like a scarecrow, and she talks to a rock. The children think she is crazy at first, but soon realize she makes school more fun, getting them to measure the room with cooked spaghetti in maths class, telling fascinating stories about a gorilla and even taking the pupils on at football.

The first book in Dominique Demers's popular series, *The New Teacher* - brilliantly illustrated by Tony Ross - is an entertaining, imaginative and inspiring book that will make you wish you had a teacher just like Miss Charlotte.

**OR, IF YOU HAVE READ *THE NEW TEACHER*,
PERHAPS YOU COULD TRY THIS ONE?**

"That beanpole of a woman!"

When the mysterious and eccentric Miss Charlotte arrives in the village of Saint-Anatole to take over the tiny library, the locals are surprised to find out that she does things differently. Wearing a long blue dress and a giant hat, she takes her books out for a walk in a wheelbarrow and shows the children that reading can be fun and useful. Sometimes she is so caught up in the magic of the stories she shares with her audience that she forgets all sense of reality - so much so that one day she loses consciousness and the children must find a way to bring her back.

The second in Dominique Demers's popular series, *The Mysterious Librarian*, brilliantly illustrated by Tony Ross, is a wonderful story about the magical and inspiring power of books.

"Let's just say I had not expected her to be that different."

Miss Charlotte - the new coach of a children's football team - has some odd methods to prepare them for the big match, including talking to the ball and drinking a special potion, smalalamiam Also, she teaches them how to lose! And to have fun Incredibly, it seems to work - but will their hopes of victory be dashed when their star player decides to join the other team?

The third in Dominique Demers's popular series, *The New Football Coach*, brilliantly illustrated by Tony Ross, is a marvellous tale about believing in yourself and beating the odds.